NGRY earth

DEADLY FLOODS

By Michael Portman

Gareth Stevens
Publishing

Please visit our website, www.garethstevens.com. For a free color catalog of all our high-quality books, call toll free 1-800-542-2595 or fax 1-877-542-2596.

Library of Congress Cataloging-in-Publication Data

Portman, Michael, 1976-
Deadly floods / Michael Portman.
    p. cm. — (Angry earth)
Includes index.
ISBN 978-1-4339-6535-7 (pbk.)
ISBN 978-1-4339-6536-4 (6-pack)
ISBN 978-1-4339-6533-3 (library binding)
1. Floods—Juvenile literature. I. Title.
GB1399.P67 2012
551.48'9—dc23

                                2011027101

First Edition

Published in 2012 by
Gareth Stevens Publishing
111 East 14th Street, Suite 349
New York, NY 10003

Copyright © 2012 Gareth Stevens Publishing

Designer: Katelyn E. Reynolds
Editor: Therese Shea

Photo credits: Cover, pp. 1, 16, 21 (inset), 24, 29 Scott Olson/Getty Images; (cover, pp. 1, 3–32 text/image box graphic) iStockphoto.com; (cover, pp. 1, 3–32 background and newspaper graphics), pp. 5, 8, 9 (inset), 10, 25 Shutterstock.com; p. 4 Stockbyte/Thinkstock; p. 6 Guillermo Legaria/AFP/Getty Images; p. 7 James Nielsen/AFP/Getty Images; p. 9 (main) Stocktrek Images/Getty Images; p. 11 Bill Hatcher/National Geographic/Getty Images; p. 12 Balint Porneczi/AFP/Getty Images; p. 13 (inset) Stock Montage/Getty Images; p. 13 (main) H. Armstrong Roberts/Retrofile/Getty Images; p. 14 David Buimovitch/AFP/Getty Images; p. 15 Warwick Sweeney/ Photographer's Choice/Getty Images; p. 17 (inset) Mike Theiss/National Geographic/Getty Images; p. 17 (main) Bradley Kanaris/Getty Images; p. 19 (inset) Scott Barbour/Getty Images; p. 19 (main) Sean Gallup/ Getty Images; pp. 20–21 Daniel Berehulak/Getty Images; p. 23 (inset) Upperhall Ltd/Robert Harding World Imagery/Getty Images; p. 23 (main) James Burke/Time & Life Pictures/ Getty Images; p. 26 Andrew Wong/ Getty Images; p. 27 (inset) Arif Ali/AFP/Getty Images; p. 27 (main) Chris Seward/Raleigh News & Observer/ MCT via Getty Images.

Printed in the United States of America

CPSIA compliance information: Batch #CW12GS: For further information contact Gareth Stevens, New York, New York at 1-800-542-2595.

CONTENTS

Words in the glossary appear in **bold** type the first time they are used in the text.

WATER WORKS

Water is one of the most important elements on Earth. Every living thing depends on water for life. People use water for drinking, cooking, cleaning, farming, and having fun. Ships and boats travel on the world's oceans, rivers, and lakes. For hundreds of years, people have used water to power machinery. Today, in many parts of the world, water is used to create electricity.

With all its important uses, it can be easy to forget just how powerful and **destructive** water can be. When rivers or lakes overflow, dams break, or ocean waves crash far onto shore, the results can be **devastating**.

Victoria Dam in Sri Lanka

Water Power

Electricity created with water is called hydroelectricity. Rushing water spins large metal blades called turbines that are connected to machines called generators. The generators create electricity that's sent to homes and businesses. Hydroelectricity is less harmful to Earth's atmosphere than fuels such as gas and coal.

◁ These turbine generators in a hydroelectric power plant turn the energy of flowing water into energy we can use to power our homes.

A flood occurs whenever water covers land that's normally dry. Flooding can happen almost anywhere in the world. Even areas that aren't close to rivers, streams, lakes, or oceans can experience flooding. In fact, floods are one of the most common natural **disasters**.

Because water is a necessary part of life, some of the most valuable and important land is near water. Many cities and towns have been built near sources of water. Millions of people live in homes that are very close to rivers and coastlines. Unfortunately, this has resulted in millions of deaths and trillions of dollars in **damage** from floods.

floodwaters cover houses in Colombia (May 2011)

Unpredictable Danger

Compared to other countries, the United States does a good job of **predicting** and preventing floods. However, US floods still cause about $6 billion worth of damage and kill about 140 people each year. In countries with less ability to predict and prevent floods, the damage is often much worse.

◁ Floodwaters brought by Hurricane Katrina cover the streets of New Orleans, Louisiana, in August 2005.

THE WATER CYCLE

Water is continuously moving on, above, and below Earth's surface. This movement is called the water cycle. The water cycle starts when heat from the sun turns water into a gas called water vapor. This process is called evaporation. The water vapor then rises into the air, where cooler temperatures turn it back into a liquid (or even ice). This process is called condensation. The liquid then combines with dust and other **particles**. These particles form clouds.

Particles in the clouds grow larger and heavier. Then the water falls back to Earth as rain, sleet, hail, or snow. This is called precipitation. Finally, the water that falls back to Earth evaporates, and the cycle begins again.

Watery Planet

The amount of water on Earth has remained the same for millions of years. The only thing that's changed is where the water is located. For example, some bodies of water have dried up, and some have formed where none existed before. Glaciers and ice sheets have melted and sent water flowing into rivers and oceans.

If you look at a picture of Earth, you can see that most of it's covered with water. Sometimes, Earth is called the "blue planet" because of this.

FALLING WATER

Several different things can happen to water that falls as precipitation. Some of the water lands in oceans, rivers, and lakes. Some of it ends up on land. Sometimes, the ground absorbs, or takes in, the water. Plants then take up some of the water absorbed by the ground. The rest may travel through the ground until it empties into a body of water.

Water that doesn't get absorbed travels across land until it reaches streams or rivers. Usually, nature does a good job of keeping the water cycle balanced. However, if there's too much water at certain points in the cycle, flooding can occur.

Drilling for Water

Not all the water that gets absorbed by the ground ends up in rivers. Some water finds its way deep underground into cracks and spaces in soil, sand, and rock. People drill wells in order to bring this "groundwater" back to the surface for drinking and other purposes.

water being drawn from a well

◁ A creek in
New Zealand
swells due to
heavy rain.

11

RIVER FLOODS

Several things can cause a river to overflow its banks. Heavy rainfall can dump more water into a river than it can hold. Melting snow, especially when combined with rain, can cause water levels to rise rapidly.

Sometimes, something blocks the steady flow of river water. Man-made dams and natural dams—such as blocks of ice, beaver dams, and logjams—can stop or greatly reduce the flow of water. When this happens, the land behind the dam will flood if water levels rise too high. If the dam breaks, a great rush of water will speed down the river all at once.

broken dam in Hungary (October 2010)

The waters of the Johnstown flood were strong enough to destroy houses and uproot trees.

▼

Johnstown, 1889

One of the worst floods in US history occurred in 1889, when a dam broke near Johnstown, Pennsylvania. After heavy rains, townspeople were warned of the coming flood. Sadly, most people thought the flood would be like others they had experienced. However, witnesses said their dam "just moved away," allowing water to destroy much of the town.

drawing of the 1889 Johnstown flood

SATURATION

Floods may also occur when the ground is saturated. "Saturation" means the ground is too wet to absorb any more water. To understand this, imagine pouring water onto a sponge. The sponge will absorb the water at first. However, once the sponge becomes completely wet, or saturated, water runs off it.

Some types of ground do a better job of absorbing water than others. Soil mixed with sand can absorb lots of water, while soil rich in clay absorbs much less. Just like a sponge, all soils reach a point where they become saturated. Extra water can result in a flood.

Desert Rains

It may be hard to believe, but deserts have some of the biggest floods! Desert sand isn't good at absorbing water quickly. Thunderstorms can fill dry rivers and lakes in a matter of minutes. As strange as it may sound, more people drown in the desert than die of thirst.

flooded road in the Negev Desert in Israel

The flooding in this field in England shows that the soil is saturated. It can't absorb any more water.

CHANGING GROUND

Soil that's frozen doesn't absorb water very well. If snow melts or it rains before frozen ground has **thawed**, water that would usually be absorbed can contribute to a flood.

Human activity can also affect how the ground absorbs water. Soil that's been plowed, such as farmland, usually isn't very good at soaking up water.

In the process of constructing cities, towns, and roads, people have covered large areas with buildings, stones, and concrete. Because these can't absorb much water, cities and towns have **drainage** systems.

floodwaters and snow surround
a North Dakota home

Man-Made Drainage

City drainage systems sometimes fail. The devastating 2005 flood of New Orleans resulting from Hurricane Katrina is one example. The drainage system in New Orleans wasn't built to carry such an immense amount of water.

◁ A nearby river flooded the city of Brisbane, Australia, in January 2011. More than 25,000 homes were affected.

FLOOD TYPES

Not all floods are alike. Some floods develop slowly and steadily. Others develop quickly, sometimes without warning. Slow, or gradual, floods may take several days to become dangerous. Gradual flooding usually means that people have enough time to get to safety. However, these floods can still cause plenty of damage. Floods that happen quickly are called flash floods. Flash floods are the most dangerous type of flood.

Flash floods can turn a calm stream or dry road into a raging river in a matter of minutes. Since flash floods happen with little or no warning, people usually don't have time to prepare for them.

Danger in a Flash

Flash floods can bring waves of water that are over 10 feet (3 m) high. In the United States, most flood-related deaths are caused by flash floods. Over half involve people in cars and trucks. Even low water can push cars off roads.

A flash flood in August 2010 quickly covered these cars in Goerlitz, Germany, near the Neisse River.

WATER OVER ROAD

sign warning of flooding in Australia

WHY ARE FLOODS DANGEROUS?

Floods are powerful. Cars, trees, bridges, and people can be swept away by the rushing currents. Water can rip buildings from their bases, causing them to fall. The resulting **debris** may be carried over large areas. Floods that cover farmland can destroy crops and drown animals. Widespread flooding may cause food shortages.

In addition to destroying property, floods can also spread sickness and disease. Floodwaters are often filled with mud, **sewage**, and poisonous chemicals. Even if a house is still standing after a flood, dirty water can cover everything, making it an unhealthy place to live.

Misleading Depths

Floodwater doesn't have to be very deep to be destructive. It may not seem like much, but just 2 feet (61 cm) of water has enough force to carry a car. It only takes 6 inches (15 cm) of rushing water to knock a person off their feet.

man using sticks to keep balance in floodwaters

Floods in Pakistan in 2010 killed more than 1,700 people and damaged or destroyed more than 1 million homes.

CAN FLOODS BE GOOD?

Not every flood is a disaster. Floodwaters can leave behind important **nutrients** that are good for soil. One example is the flooding of the Nile River in Egypt. For thousands of years, Egyptians depended on the seasonal flooding of the Nile to **fertilize** their soil. Farmers looked forward to the heavy rains that caused the Nile to flood.

In 1970, a dam was built on the Nile River to control the water flow. Water is let out as it's needed. This has allowed the planting season to last all year, resulting in more food.

Mixing of the Waters

The Nile River flows from south to north and empties into the Mediterranean Sea. The water level in the Mediterranean Sea has been rising over the years. If the sea's salty water rises too high, it could flood the northern part of Egypt, destroying valuable farmland and **contaminating** drinking water.

Egypt's Aswan High Dam on the Nile River

The Aswan High Dam controls the Nile's waters and created Lake Nasser, shown here. The dam is also a source of hydroelectric power.

CAN FLOODS BE CONTROLLED?

For thousands of years, people have been trying to control floods. They build dams to control the flow of water. They build walls, called levees, to keep rivers from overflowing. They build tunnels and concrete channels to move water from one place to another. Sometimes the efforts are successful. Other times, they have disastrous effects.

If dams and levees aren't tall enough, rising floodwaters can overflow them. If they're old or poorly made, water pressure can cause them to break. Dams, levees, and channels may prevent flooding in one area but direct water into other areas, causing flooding there.

people in North Dakota building a levee

There's enough concrete in the Hoover Dam to pave a highway from New York City to San Francisco, California. ▼

A Concrete Giant

The Hoover Dam is one of the most famous dams in the United States. It stretches across the Colorado River between Arizona and Nevada. Besides controlling flooding along the river, the Hoover Dam also creates hydroelectricity.

FLOODS AROUND THE WORLD

China has had some of the worst floods in history. Many of those floods took place on China's biggest river, the Yangtze. In June 2011, following months of dry weather, heavy rains caused the Yangtze River to flood once again.

In summer 2010, Pakistan suffered one of the worst natural disasters in recent history. Flooding devastated large areas of the country. Nearly 20 million people were affected; many of them lost their homes.

In spring 2011, heavy rains and melting snow caused the Mississippi River, the largest river in the United States, to experience record-breaking floods. The waters forced thousands of people in several states to flee their homes.

Three Gorges Dam

The Three Gorges Dam in China is the world's largest hydroelectric dam. It was built both to produce electricity and to reduce flooding on the Yangtze River. Construction began in 1992 and was completed in 2006. Recently, the dam has been blamed for water shortages in some parts of China.

Three Gorges Dam

2010 floods in Pakistan

When Hurricane Irene blew onto the East Coast in August 2011, it caused severe damage and flooding from North Carolina to Maine and into Canada. Roads, houses, and crops were destroyed. Millions were without electricity or transportation for days.

FLOOD SAFETY

Since floods can happen almost anywhere, it's important to be prepared. Here's a list of important steps to follow:

- Listen to television and radio reports to stay informed of a flood's progress. (Battery-powered radios are best in case electricity is cut off.)

- If there's danger of a flash flood in your area, be sure to get to higher ground.

- Don't try to cross moving water on foot or in a car.

- Even if the water isn't flowing very fast, it may contain things that will make you sick.

- After a flood, return to your house only after you've been told it's safe.

Ready to Rescue

Local police, fire departments, and rescue forces are usually first on the scene during a flood. If necessary, the National Guard or US Army may be called in to help as well. It's a good idea to carefully follow the instructions of rescue workers as well as local health departments during and after a flood.

Law enforcement officers keep an eye on homes and look for people to rescue during and after severe floods like this one along the Mississippi River.

GLOSSARY

contaminate: to pollute something

damage: harm. Also, to cause harm.

debris: pieces of something that has been destroyed or broken

destructive: causing damage

devastating: causing widespread damage

disaster: an event that causes serious loss or destruction

drainage: a system of pipes or channels that carry water or sewage away from a place

fertilize: to add something to soil to increase its ability to grow plants

nutrient: something a living thing needs to grow and stay alive

particle: a very small bit of something

predict: to guess what will happen in the future based on facts or knowledge

sewage: waste matter from buildings that is carried away through sewers

thaw: to melt

FOR MORE INFORMATION

Books

Ceban, Bonnie J. *Floods and Mudslides: Disaster & Survival.* Berkeley Heights, NJ: Enslow Publishers, 2005.

Doeden, Matt. *How to Survive a Flood.* Mankato, MN: Capstone Press, 2009.

Woods, Michael, and Mary B. Woods. *Floods.* Minneapolis, MN: Lerner Publications, 2007.

Websites

FEMA Ready Kids
www.ready.gov/kids/home.html
Learn how to create an emergency kit for your home.

How Floods Work
science.howstuffworks.com/nature/natural-disasters/flood.htm
Read much more about water and floods, and see pictures of famous floods.

INDEX